A PROMISE
AT THE ALAMO

The Story of a Texas Girl

Maria Hernandez

A PROMISE
AT THE ALAMO

The Story of a Texas Girl

BY DOROTHY AND THOMAS HOOBLER

AND CAREY-GREENBERG ASSOCIATES

PICTURES BY JENNIFER HEWITSON

SILVER BURDETT PRESS

**Library of Congress Cataloging-
in-Publication Data**
Hoobler, Dorothy.
A promise at the Alamo : the story of a Texas girl /
by Dorothy and Thomas Hoobler
and Carey-Greenberg Associates.
    p.   cm.—(Her story)
Summary: A San Antonio girl and her family
are caught up in the Battle of the Alamo in 1836.
    1. Alamo (San Antonio, Tex.)—Siege,
    1836—Juvenile fiction. [1. Alamo
    (San Antonio, Tex.)—Siege, 1836—Fiction.
    2. Texas—History—To 1846—Fiction.]
I. Hoobler, Thomas.   II. Carey-Greenberg Associates.
    III. Title.   IV. Series.
    PZ7.H76227Pr   1992
    90-26584   CIP   AC
ISBN 0-382-24147-9 (LSB)   10 9 8 7 6 5 4 3 2
ISBN 0-382-24352-8 (PBK)   10 9 8 7 6 5 4 3 2

CONTENTS

CHAPTER ONE

Feliz Navidad!

MARIA HERNANDEZ knocked at the door of the house. Immediately a voice behind it called, "Who's there?"

"We are travelers," Maria replied, "without a place to stay. We only want a place to rest." Her six-year-old brother, José, squeezed her hand tightly. He was so excited, he could hardly wait for his turn.

"Go away!" the voice behind the door said. "Don't bother us. We have no room!"

"We're cold and tired," Maria pleaded. "We have come from far away!"

"But I don't know you. Who are you?"

Maria nudged José, and he piped up, "I am Jo-

seph of Nazareth, a carpenter, and with me is
Mary, my wife. She will soon give birth to the
Son of God."

Someone behind them giggled, and others
whispered, "Hush!"

The door opened, and Señora Garcia smiled
down at them. "Then come into my humble
home," she said. "And may the Lord give shelter
to my soul when I leave this world."

Maria and José stepped through the doorway,
followed by all the other children from their
street. Señora Garcia led them to the *naci-*
miento that her family had prepared. It was a
model of the stable in which Jesus had been
born. Little clay figures of Mary, Joseph, baby Jesus, and the shepherds stood inside it. Señora
Garcia had decorated the stable with flowers
and grasses.

The children began to sing the old hymn that
told of the travels of Mary and Joseph. When they
finished, they knelt and prayed that God would
not close the doors of heaven to them.

Then everybody stood and eagerly looked
around. Señora Garcia laughed. "Are you ex-
pecting something else?" she said.

They knew she was only joking, and of course
she waved them into the next room. There it

was: the *piñata*, hanging from a hook on the ceiling. She had made one that looked like a bull, with horns and a fierce face with a ring through its nose. Everyone clapped and cheered.

Señora Garcia brought an old broomstick. "Now, who's the youngest?" she said. The children pushed little Victoria, who was only four, to the front. Maria blindfolded her, spun her around gently, and gave her a nudge.

Victoria swung wildly in the air with the broomstick while the others shouted and told her which way to go. Señora Garcia loosened the rope that held the piñata and lowered it so that it hung right in front of Victoria.

"Swing! Swing!" the others called. Finally she hit it so hard that she fell backward on the floor. She jumped up and pushed the blindfold off. "It's not broken!" she said, disappointed.

But that was part of the fun. Each child got to take a turn, for the piñata was strong. Soon, though, someone made a crack in it, and a few pieces of candy fell out. They were quickly grabbed up, and another child was blindfolded. A few more cracks appeared in the piñata, but no more candy fell out.

By the time it was Maria's turn, she knew the

piñata was ready to break. Blindfolded, she stepped forward and took a big swing. She missed, but felt the broomstick brush the side of the piñata. Now she knew where it was, and took a deep breath. Then she swung the stick with all her might.

She felt the piñata shatter, and heard the shower of candies, fruits, and trinkets that clattered on the floor. A great shout went up, and she was nearly knocked over as the other children scrambled around her feet. She snatched off the blindfold and joined them.

Señora Garcia brought out a jug of guava juice and poured cups of it for all the children. José sat down happily, his mouth and pockets stuffed with candy. "Your house tomorrow," the other children reminded Maria.

For this was only the first of the nine nights before Christmas. Each night the children of the neighborhood went to a different house. One girl and one boy played the parts of Mary and Joseph searching for a place to stay. In the Bible story, it had taken them nine days to travel from Nazareth to Bethlehem. And in the year 1835, nine houses in every street of San Antonio, Texas, prepared a nacimiento and piñata for the visitors.

"What does your piñata look like?" Maria's friend Estrella asked.

"Oh, it's a secret," Maria said.

The next day she and José helped put the finishing touches on their family's piñata. The figure was their father's idea. They put a rope around its neck and hung it from the ceiling.

Maria laughed. Her father nodded. "Everyone will know him," he said. It was a model of General Cós, the commander of the Mexican troops who had just been driven out of San Antonio a week earlier.

Maria's mother wagged her finger. "If General Cós ever returns, and someone tells about this, we will have trouble."

Señor Hernandez snorted. "We have driven him out of Texas for good. Sam Houston and my friend Jim Bowie—you saw how they fought. And so did General Cós. He is afraid of the Texans now."

"You fought bravely too, Papa," said Maria.

"Ah yes, we all did. We fought for our homes, for our children, for the right to be free. You know, before you were born, I fought against the Spanish too. Fifteen years ago, to win Mexico's freedom." He sighed. "But then Santa Anna took control of Mexico. I did not fight the Spanish only to live under a dictator."

"Perhaps Santa Anna will come here," said Mama. "He will be stronger than General Cós."

Papa shook his head. "It is a long way from his palace in Mexico City," he said.

Mama still looked worried.

But the children who came to their house that night all laughed when they saw General Cós hanging high above the floor. The children swung at him as bravely as their fathers had. And they cheered when he fell.

At midnight on Christmas Eve, the Hernandezes joined the rest of the town at the high mass in the cathedral of San Fernando. The church was filled with the smell of incense and the sounds of the choir singing joyfully of the birth of Jesus. *"Feliz Navidad!"* they sang—"Merry Christmas!" That year there was a special reason for celebrating. It looked as if Texas would now be free.

Mama took Maria to the side altar, where dozens of candles burned. Mama lit one more and motioned for her daughter to kneel with her. "Pray," she said. "Pray that there will be no more fighting, and that Santa Anna will leave us alone here."

Maria knelt and bowed her head. But she knew that her mother worried for nothing. Maria thought of Jim Bowie. No one could defeat him!

The children of San Antonio now eagerly awaited the final day of the Christmas season—January 6, 1836, the Feast of the Wise Men. On that day the three Wise Men from the East had brought gifts for Jesus, and so Mexican children were given their Christmas presents then.

Maria helped her mother bake the special cake for the feast day. They put a little plaster statue of Jesus inside before baking it in the oven. "Will Jim Bowie come to share our cake?" Maria asked.

"Perhaps," said Mama. "I fear the Navidad celebrations make him sad. Do you remember his wife?"

"Oh yes, Mama—such a beautiful woman."

"Yes. She was the daughter of the vice-governor of Texas. The whole town came to their wedding, and there was a grand fiesta. Soon she gave him two children. But then, God took them all away when the cholera disease swept through the town." Mama glanced at Maria and crossed herself.

"Jim Bowie was not here when they died," Mama continued. "He had gone to the United States on business. When he returned, and they told him . . . it was a terrible thing. He shut himself in his big house all alone and stayed there a long time. Since then, he is a changed man. I fear that he fights so bravely because he looks for death."

"Oh, Mama," said Maria. "That is so sad."

"Yes, and so if he does not want to be around children on such a day of joy, you will understand."

But Jim Bowie surprised them. He came to the Hernandez house on the Day of the Wise Men, bringing gifts for Maria and José. Wonderful presents—a rocking horse and a beautiful doll!

Bowie smiled as they opened the gifts, but when Maria hugged him, she saw the sadness in his eyes. She wished she could make him happier. "Mama and I baked a cake for the Wise Men's feast," she said. "Will you share it with us?"

"I'd love some," he said.

Maria brought out the cake and carefully cut a piece for everyone. As their guest, Bowie was served first. He bit into the cake and then stopped. Carefully, he put it down on his plate.

He had the piece with the little statue of Jesus baked into it!

"Hola!" José said. "You know what that means?"

"Hush," Mama whispered. "It is only a custom," she explained, but Bowie waved his hand and smiled.

"I know what it means," he said. "Now I must invite everyone here to a fiesta at my house."

"You don't have to do that," said Mama.

"Of course I will," Bowie said. He looked at José. "But we must wait until we're sure that Santa Anna will not interrupt our fiesta."

"General Cós promised he would not return to Texas," Maria said.

"But Santa Anna didn't promise," Bowie said. "Sam Houston thinks he's going to bring an army here. A lot of these new settlers from the United States are eager to fight him. They want Texas to be part of the U.S."

"But you are from the United States too," Maria pointed out.

Bowie replied, "When I came here, I agreed to live under Mexico's laws. I kept my part of the bargain—until Santa Anna changed the laws."

Maria was curious. She asked Bowie, "Do you feel more like a Mexican or an Americano?"

He smiled. "Tell you the truth, I think of myself as a Texan now."

"So do I," Papa said. "And if Santa Anna is smart, he will leave Texas alone."

CHAPTER TWO

"We'll Stand Here"

SAM HOUSTON seemed to be right. In the next two weeks, rumors swept the town of San Antonio. Santa Anna was said to be marching north to Texas with a large army. Many of the townspeople were afraid, for they knew that Santa Anna was far crueler than General Cós had been.

But Papa simply shrugged and said, "If we must fight again, we will." Papa was the town's blacksmith, and Bowie asked him to fix up the cannons that General Cós had left behind. Maria and Jośe went to the Alamo with them.

The Alamo was an old Spanish mission north of town. It had been abandoned long ago, but its strong walls made it a good place for a fort. General Cós had begun to rebuild it, but the Texans had attacked before he finished.

Papa pointed to the big gap in the southeast corner of the wall. "We must fix that, or Santa Anna's men will come marching through," Papa said.

Bowie nodded. "If we get enough people to help, we can build a wall of earth there."

"It will take time," replied Papa.

"We should have plenty of time," said Bowie. "If Santa Anna does come, he won't be here till summer. How about the cannons?"

"They are in good shape," said Papa. "But we will need cannonballs, and as many soldiers as Sam Houston can send us."

"Get started," said Bowie. "I'll ride to Washington-on-the-Brazos and tell Sam Houston what the situation is."

In the days that followed, Bowie's soldiers and the townsfolk set to work. They cut down trees and set thick posts in the gap in the Alamo wall. Then they began to bring carts of earth to pile around the posts. Others hauled the heavy cannons to the top of the walls.

Maria was busy in Papa's blacksmith shop. People brought all the scrap iron they could find for him to melt down into cannonballs. She had to keep the fire in the forge going with firewood. It was hot, sweaty work, but she was used to it. And everybody else was needed to help fortify the Alamo.

She watched as Papa carefully ladled the bubbling metal into the mold for the cannonballs. Later, when they cooled, the balls were loaded onto a cart and taken to the fort. "We're doing well," Papa said at the end of one of the long days. He patted Maria on the back. "Santa Anna isn't going to take San Antonio away from us."

Then, on January 18, Jim Bowie returned. Maria saw him ride up outside the smithy. He got off his horse slowly, and she saw that he had become thinner. When he came into the shop, the smoke got into his lungs, and he began to cough. She rushed forward, "You're sick," she said.

"Just a cold," he said. "It's been a cold winter."

"Come into the house," she told him. "Mama is making chili."

He followed her inside. When Mama brought him a bowl of chili, Maria saw his hands shake as he spooned it into his mouth. It worried her.

Then Papa came through the door, wiping his hands with a cloth. "How many men did you bring?" he asked Bowie.

"Only thirty," Bowie said.

Papa nodded. "And when will the rest arrive?"

Bowie shook his head sadly. "Houston can't spare any more. I have bad news, my friend. Houston has ordered me to blow up the Alamo."

Papa was thunderstruck. "But . . . why?"

"Houston thinks we should abandon the town. He hasn't got a big enough army to defend it. He figures that we ought to let Santa Anna take San Antonio while we wait for more volunteers. There's a lot of people coming from the United States, he says."

"But that's impossible," said Papa. "Santa Anna will burn the town in revenge. We will lose our homes, our shops . . . everything!"

"I know," said Bowie. "My home too." He looked out the window, and Maria saw his eyes go far away. Was he thinking of the days when his wife and children lived in the fine big house with him?

Bowie stood up suddenly. "Well," he said. "No hurry about it, is there? Let's look at the progress that you've made." Bowie inspected the work that had been done at the fort and nodded approvingly. Nothing more was said about blowing up the Alamo.

When Papa saw that his friend was sick, he invited Bowie to stay at their house. But Bowie said he didn't want to bother them. So every night Mama sent Maria with some food for him. "He's not eating right," Mama said. "You can see that he doesn't take care of himself."

The first time, Maria knocked at the door of Bowie's big house. When no one answered, she shyly went inside anyway. She found Bowie sitting in front of an empty fireplace, staring at the wall above the mantle. Hanging there was a small painting of a woman and two children. Maria didn't need to ask who they were.

She apologized for disturbing him, but he asked her to stay while he ate. And she did, every night. He enjoyed having someone to talk to, and told her stories. The time he rode an alligator to death. Sailing on a pirate ship with Jean Lafitte. The big fight when he and ten friends fought off a hundred Indians who wanted his silver mine.

He didn't seem to notice when the sun went down and shadows fell across the room. But Maria got up and lit candles, because it was too scary listening to these stories in the dark.

At the beginning of February, two more groups of soldiers arrived in San Antonio. The first was led by Colonel William Travis. Maria

was in the street with Jim Bowie as Travis passed by on his horse. Travis wore a big white hat and red pantaloons. "Looks like a dandy, doesn't he?" Bowie said. "Used to be a lawyer, but he can fight like a tiger."

Travis immediately took command of the forces at the Alamo. Like Bowie, he disagreed with Houston's plan to abandon the Alamo. He had come to fight, and that made everybody feel safer.

A few days later, Maria was working at the forge when she heard a big commotion in the street. People were shouting and laughing. When she looked out the window, she saw a crowd of people around a tall, thin man on horseback. He wore a fur cap with a tail hanging down in back; it looked like he had scooped up a raccoon and placed it on his head.

"Well now, we goin' to fight or we goin' to party?" the man shouted. He drew a long rifle from the leather sheath on his horse. "Here's my Old Betsy! Who wants to fight?"

"Santa Anna's not here yet!" someone in the crowd shouted.

"Good thing for him," the horseman replied. "So we'll party then!" He reached into one of his big saddlebags and took out a fiddle. He set it on his shoulder and began to play, making music of a kind Maria had never heard before.

"What you folks call your big parties down here?" the man said. "A feestie?"

"A fiesta!" the crowd cheered back at him.

"I like the sound o' that! So you all tell everybody that Davy Crockett's here with a dozen genuine Tennessee bear hunters, and we want a dang big fee-est-ee!"

"Crockett's here?" Jim Bowie said when Maria took him his supper that night. "If he's half as good as people say, we're lucky to have him."

"The people are going to have a fiesta for him tonight," Maria said.

"Well, then we'll go," Bowie said. He got up from his chair, but he nearly fell and Maria rushed to hold his arm. He shook her off. "Slipped," he muttered. But he walked slowly as they made their way to the Plaza de las Islas, the big open square in front of the cathedral.

They heard the music and singing before they got there. It really was a joyful fiesta. When Crockett played his fiddle, it made people's feet start to tap. Maria's eyes widened as she saw her Papa and Mama among those who were dancing to the strange Tennessee music.

After a while, Crockett sat down and some of the young men of the town began to play flamenco dances on their guitars. Jim Bowie walked over to Crockett, and Maria followed.

"Congressman Crockett?" Bowie said.

Crockett looked up. His eyes narrowed for a second, but then he laughed. "Not no more," he said. "I told the people of Tennessee that if they voted me out of Congress, they could go to blazes and I would go to Texas. So they did, and here I am. And you're Jim Bowie, I reckon." He pointed to the big knife that Bowie always wore on his belt. "Only one man uses a knife like that."

Bowie shook hands. "We're glad to have you."

"I heard you was here," Crockett said. "That's why I headed for San Antone. Like to be next to somebody I can count on in a real fight."

"Houston wants us to abandon the town," Bowie said.

"But you ain't done that," said Crockett.

"We'll stand here," Bowie replied. "The Alamo is as good a fort as we've got, and Santa Anna is likely to attack here first. If we get enough men, we can stop him."

Crockett shrugged. "Glad that's settled," he said. "Nothing to do but wait, so we may's well dance. Might never get the chance again." He stood up and looked at Maria. "You know how to dance, little gal?"

Maria did, but she shook her head wildly.

Crockett just laughed. "Easy as slidin' off a frog's back." He bent over and put his arm around her waist. Then he swooped her off her feet and whirled her into the center of the plaza. He paid no attention to the music. He just stamped his feet and carried Maria with him. Round and round they went, spinning past the people in the crowd.

Maria decided later that she had never had such a good time in her life.

CHAPTER THREE

"Victory or Death!"

THOUGH CROCKETT had only brought twelve riflemen with him, he raised everybody's spirits. During the day he sat in the main square and told stories to the little children like José.

José repeated them all at home. "Do you know how he got that fur cap he always wears? He said that he chased a raccoon up a tree. But when the raccoon saw him aim Old Betsy, he climbed down the tree and gave up!"

Of course Maria didn't believe that, but Papa said it was true that Davy Crockett really had been a member of the Congress of the United States. "Hola!" said Maria. "Are there so many Americanos as crazy as him?"

"They say he can shoot better than any man alive," said José.

"Not better than Jim Bowie," Maria replied.

Papa smiled at her. "Bowie respects him," he said. "And when people hear that Crockett is here, more soldiers will come, for they will want their share of glory."

But a few days later a scout returned with bad news. "Santa Anna has already crossed the Rio Grande," he reported. "He will be here in less than a week."

The news threw the townspeople into a panic. They knew that there were not enough soldiers to defend the Alamo. Some families abandoned their homes that very day, put their belongings into wagons, and headed east for Gonzales.

That evening at supper Jim Bowie appeared in the doorway. Mama made him sit down and gave him a plate of tacos, but he didn't eat. "Tomorrow we're going to move all the troops into the Alamo," he told them.

He looked at Papa. "You have a family. No one will hold it against you if you stay in your home. Some of the townspeople believe that Santa Anna will not harm them if they welcome him."

"I will never bow my head to the dictator," Papa said. "I can fight as well as anyone, and you will need someone to repair the cannons." Papa looked at his friend and said, "I will join you."

"Then you should send your wife and children to safety," said Bowie. Papa nodded.

But then Mama spoke up, surprising everyone. "What place is safe while Santa Anna is in Texas?" she said. "If we leave, who can tell what will happen to us on the road? We will never rest, for we will always be worrying about you."

Maria saw determination in her mother's eyes. "If you men are brave enough to fight," Mama said, "then we should be brave enough to stand by you. We will go to the Alamo too."

Maria hugged her mother. Bowie and Papa glanced at each other. "They will not be the only ones," Bowie said.

That was true. The next day, when they moved into the Alamo, several other women and children joined them. Susanna Dickinson, whose husband was an Americano officer, brought her infant daughter. She and Maria's mother helped get everyone settled inside the old Alamo chapel. Though its roof had fallen in years before, its walls were thicker than any other part of the fort. Santa Anna's cannons would not be able to break them down.

It was a spooky place. The sunlight high above

cast dark shadows through the broken beams of the ruined roof. Maria shivered as she saw a rat scurry into the rubble that covered the floor. She noticed a ladder leaning against one of the walls, and while Mama was busy, she climbed up.

There, on top of the walls, stood one of the big cannons. Not far away, she saw Davy Crockett. He waved her over. The wall was wide enough so that she could easily walk along it.

"Ready for another dance?" he asked.

"How can you joke when Santa Anna's coming?" Maria asked.

"Wal, he ain't gonna come tippy-toe, sneaky-like in the dark. We'll have plenty of warning, you can bet."

He pointed to the front of the fort, where the wall of earth had been built. "Travis said keep Santa Anna's boys off that wall. So I will. Might keep an eye on them women and kids in the church, Travis said too."

"Don't worry about us," she said.

He smiled. "Jim Bowie said you was a good, brave gal. You want to help?"

She nodded eagerly, and he showed her how to make the little paper packets of gunpowder for his rifle. He used a rod to push one down the

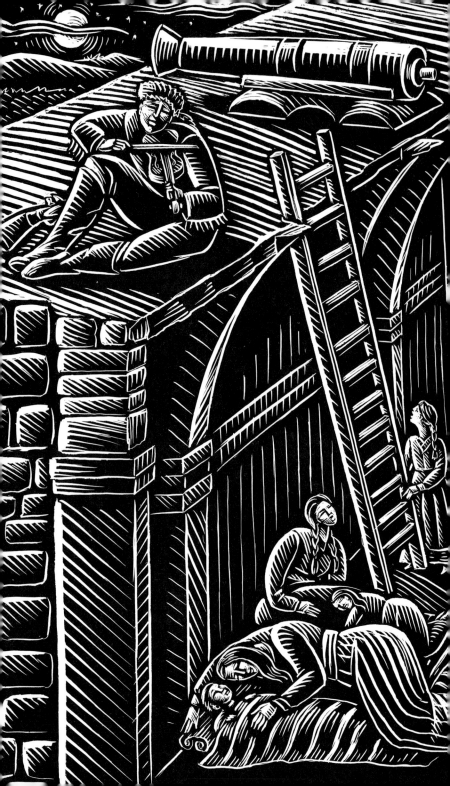

barrel with a bullet. "No time to make them when the battle starts," he explained.

So Maria set to work, and got José and some of the other children to help. Before long they had hundreds of powder loads for Crockett and his men.

It was good to be doing something, for the waiting was hard. A sentry stood in the church tower in town, ready to give the alarm if Santa Anna appeared in the distance. People brought cattle and corn into the fort, so that those inside would not starve. Everybody still hoped that more volunteers would arrive before Santa Anna did.

At night Maria found it hard to fall asleep. Every time she heard a horse moving outside, she sat up. Then she heard the sounds of Crockett's fiddle playing softly up above. He was awake too, waiting in the dark. And at last she felt safe enough to close her eyes.

Jim Bowie's illness had gotten worse. One day he just keeled over on the ground and had to be carried to a room in the south barracks. It was just across the plaza from the church, and Maria rushed to him when she heard the news.

He was feverish and kept trying to rise from his cot. A young woman had come to tend him, and with Maria's help she got him to lie still.

Bowie looked miserably at Maria. "I thought I had more time," he said. "Now, I'm just a burden."

"No, no," she said. "Everyone believes in you. More soldiers will come because you're here."

"Travis hopes so," he said. "He keeps sending messages, asking for help." He took her hand. "Maria, there's one thing I'd like to have."

"What is it?"

"You know that painting in my house? The one of my wife and children?"

"Oh yes. Where you always sit."

He nodded. "Could you bring it here? I'd like to be able to look on it again if I'm going to die."

"You won't die," Maria said. "Don't talk like that. I promise you. I will bring the picture."

But as she went outside, a bugle blew. People hurried to close the gate at the entrance to the fort. She ran toward them. "Wait!" she said. "I want to go out!"

"Get back!" they shouted at her. "Didn't you hear the signal? Santa Anna has arrived."

Maria rushed to the top of the wall. Crockett stood there, looking off into the distance. He pointed. "Mighty purty outfits," he said.

Far off on the other side of San Antonio, she saw a long line of mounted horsemen wear-

ing shiny metal breastplates and blue trousers.
Behind them marched soldiers in dusty white
uniforms. "Now we'll see if they can shoot,"
Crockett said.

Early the next morning Papa come to the
chapel. "Santa Anna's men are bringing up their
cannons," he said. He and Captain Dickinson
climbed the ladder to the wall, preparing to fire
the cannon there.

Maria begged her mother to let her go up too,
but Mama absolutely refused. "We can only pray
now," she said.

Soon they heard the sounds of rifle shots from
the place where Crockett and his men stood.
Then came the boom of a cannon, but it was far
off. A great thud caused everyone to jump. A can-
nonball had struck the wall, but it failed to break
through!

Another cannon roared—the one on the roof.
Then another and another along the front wall.
Maria felt proud as she realized that the Alamo's
defenders were fighting with some of the cannonballs she had helped to make.

That gave her an idea. She began to make
some more of the powder loads for Crockett
and his men. But she ached with frustration that
she could not see what was going on.

That morning the battle was a short one. In

half an hour, the gunfire stopped, and Maria could hear shouts of joy from the roof.

Maria couldn't control herself any longer. She scooped up the pile of powder loads and ran for the ladder. Mama called to her, but Maria was already halfway up.

She poked her head outside. Papa and Captain Dickinson, their faces sooty with powder, were cheering. Maria saw some of Santa Anna's men lying on the ground by their cannons. Most of the rest were running back to the town.

She boosted herself up to the wall. When Papa did not tell her to go back, she ran to Crockett. "We've won!" she said.

He shook his head. "Just for today." He grinned when he saw she had brought him more ammunition. "Good thinkin'," he said. He took one of them and stuffed it down his rifle barrel. "Look at that fool," he said. "He don't know it's over."

One of Santa Anna's officers was still trying to fire one of the cannons. He was so far away that Maria could barely see the gold braid on the shoulders of his coat. But Crockett aimed his rifle and pulled the trigger.

Bang! The officer's tall black hat flew off his head. Maria gasped. "I never saw anyone shoot as good as you."

"Aw, I count that a miss," he said. The officer, minus his hat, was running down the hill after the others. "He got away."

The next day they could see a red flag flying from the bell tower of the church in town. "It is a signal from Santa Anna," Papa told Maria. "It means that he will give no quarter, take no prisoners. Now we must resist, or die."

He looked at Maria. "Do not worry. Help is sure to come soon. Travis will send another message to Houston tonight."

Everyone inside the Alamo gathered in the plaza to hear Travis read the message aloud. He began it, "To the People of Texas and all Americans in the world." Maria didn't understand all the big words he used, but she could tell it was a very brave message. "I shall never surrender or retreat," Travis read. At the end, he shouted the final words: "Victory or Death!"

A hush fell over the crowd for a moment. Then Davy Crockett yelled, "Victory or Death!" too, and everybody else joined in.

But that night Maria lay awake for a long time thinking of the words. Would it be victory? Or death? For the first time, she began to feel afraid.

CHAPTER FOUR

A Line in the Dust

THERE WERE NO more battles in the next few
days. Some of Santa Anna's men came as close as
they dared and shouted insults. When Crockett
and his men shot at them, they ran away again.
"Santa Anna ain't got enough men to take us
head on," Crockett told Maria. "But the scouts
say he's got lots more on the way. Then they'll
come at us from all sides."

Jim Bowie was still sick, and when Maria vis-
ited him, he only nodded when she told him
that help was coming soon. He said no more
about the picture he had asked for, but she had
not forgotten.

One night she waited until she was sure

everyone else was asleep, and then carefully climbed the ladder in the dark. The front gate was always closed, but she knew she could slide down the front wall. It would be no more difficult than climbing a steep hill.

But as she tiptoed along the wall, someone grabbed her arm. It was Crockett of course. He seemed never to sleep. "Where you think you're goin'?" he asked.

"I have to get something for Jim Bowie," she said. She explained about the picture.

Crockett thought for a moment. "Mighty silly thing to risk your life for," he said.

"You risked your life by coming here," she pointed out. "Why?"

He chuckled. "Seemed like a good idea at the time. Aw well, one fool deserves another. I don't think Santa Anna's sentries are any too careful. Sounds to me like they party half the night, and now they'll mostly be asleep. You look sharp, hear? If anybody stops you, tell 'em you belong to somebody in town. I'll wait up for you."

Maria went over the wall and hurried toward the town. The moon was hidden behind clouds, and the streets were pitch-black. Even so, she knew the way well enough to follow it in the dark.

She had to pass through the city's main square to get to Bowie's house. Santa Anna's men had set up their tents here. A few campfires were burning low. She counted them and realized that Santa Anna truly did not have as many soldiers as she had expected.

She slipped down a narrow street. At the other end, two lanterns hung outside a *cantina*. She could hear laughter and singing inside. She crossed to the other side of the street, out of the light.

Then she tripped and fell over a man who was lying on the ground. She had not seen him. He grunted and grabbed for her, but she scrambled out of his reach. "Who's that?" he called, and she realized he was drunk.

"I'm looking for my papa," she said. "Have you seen him?"

"Get out of my way," he mumbled, trying to get to his feet. She ran on into the darkness.

At last she came to Bowie's house. The soldiers had not disturbed it. She needed no light to find the painting, and carefully lifted it from the wall. It was not heavy, and she hurried back to the fort with it.

Crockett was waiting. He dropped a rope over the wall, and as she held it he pulled her back

up. "So you got it," he said. "Maybe that's a sign o' good luck."

In the morning she took the painting to Jim Bowie. His eyes lit up when he saw it, and she could see how much it meant to him. She hung it on the wall of his room where he could see it from his bed. She noticed that he now kept two pistols by his side.

That afternoon the men on the wall began to shout. Maria thought that Santa Anna was attacking again. But then the gate was opened, and a group of riders galloped inside. Maria's heart soared when she saw them. Help at last! she thought.

The men had come from the town of Gonzales. But there were only thirty-two of them, and they reported that the town could not spare more. People there worried that Santa Anna would attack them next.

Even so, it was an encouraging sign. "Many more will come now," Maria told her mother. But Mama still seemed to be worried. "We will be all right," Maria insisted.

Mama took her aside so that José could not hear. "Your Papa was here earlier," she told Maria. "Travis has told him they need someone to ride to Sam Houston and ask for his help. Your

Papa knows better than anyone else the quickest way to get there." She looked at Maria to make sure she understood. Maria nodded.

"Your papa does not want to leave us here," Mama said. "He cannot make up his mind."

"Tell him to go, Mama," Maria said quietly. "We will be safe. I saw—" She bit her tongue. She could not tell Mama that she had seen Santa Anna did not have enough soldiers to attack, for then Mama would know she had left the fort. "I saw how well Crockett and his men can shoot. They will keep us safe. Papa must be the one to go."

Mama nodded. "I have already told him," she said. "He leaves tonight. He will take Jim Bowie's horse."

Mama allowed Maria to climb the ladder to watch Papa go. She sat on the wall next to Crockett, and they heard the gate creak open. Papa led the horse out, walking beside it to make as little noise as possible. He looked back one time, and Maria waved, hoping he could see her. But he made no sign, and soon disappeared in the darkness.

"He'll get through," Crockett told her. "You'll see. He'll be back in a few days."

"Do you really think so?" she asked.

He sat silently for a moment, and then said, "I always say be sure you're right, then go ahead. You sure he's right to go?"

"Oh yes."

"Well then, you can be proud of him. Keep that in your mind, whatever happens. But keep makin' powder loads."

Every day Maria thought about Papa. She tried to figure how far he might have ridden by then. And how many days till he returned. She found excuses to go up on the wall, taking water and food to Crockett and his men, so that she could look off in the distance. Come soon! she thought. Come soon!

But on March 3, the people in the Alamo heard shouts coming from the town. Almost everyone rushed to the wall then, hoping that Houston had come at last.

But their hopes were crushed. What they saw was a line of Mexican soldiers—Santa Anna's reinforcements. "Must be more than a thousand of them," Crockett muttered. "We don't even have two hundred."

The defenders of the Alamo watched helplessly as Santa Anna made his preparations. For two days his soldiers moved into position on all sides of the fort. They stayed at a safe distance, but everyone could see that they were planning to attack.

On the morning of March 5, Travis called everyone outside. They gathered in the big dusty courtyard. Even Jim Bowie asked to be carried outside on a stretcher.

Finally, Travis began to speak. "You all can see what is happening," he said. "Santa Anna may attack at any time. The odds against us are great. I cannot ask anyone to give up his life in vain. I have sworn not to surrender the fort, but the choice must be yours."

He pulled his sword from his belt and drew a line in the dust with it. "I stand here," he said on one side of the line. "Anyone who chooses to stay with me can cross the line."

People began to look at each other. Then, one by one, they began to step over the line. Crockett was first, Maria saw.

But others hesitated. Then Jim Bowie called out, in a voice that was weak, but loud enough for all to hear. "Who will carry me across?" he said. Two of his friends picked up his stretcher and gently lifted him over the line with them.

The women and children were off to the side,

but Maria pulled away from Mama and ran to Bowie's side. José was right behind her. People laughed, a little embarrassed, but then Mama and Mrs. Dickinson with her baby joined them. The rest of the women and children followed.

In the end, only one man refused. His name was Ross, and Maria was glad he was not a Mexican. That night he slipped over the wall and she never saw him again.

The defenders of the Alamo had made their decision, and for the rest of the day they worked silently, readying the fort for the battle to come. Maria went to Jim Bowie's room, but before she could speak, he said, "Crockett told me how you brought this painting here. You should not have done that."

"I promised you," she said.

He nodded. "Your parents are lucky to have such a daughter. I wish that I could have seen—" His voice caught, and he looked away for a second. Then he reached for her hand, closing his big fist around it tightly.

"Promise me one more thing," he said.

She nodded, afraid to speak for fear that she would burst into tears.

"I believe Santa Anna will spare the women and children," he said. "If you get away from here, think of me sometimes. I would like to have someone to remember me."

"I will *never* forget you," she said. "And I will tell others about you so that no one will ever forget. They will remember, I promise."

He let her hand slip from his. She turned away, for she did not want him to see her crying.

That night Mama made Maria sleep next to her. Mama knew she had been going up to the roof, and told her it was too dangerous tonight. So she never got to wish Davy Crockett good luck, but as she lay in the dark she heard the scratchy sound of his fiddle. What a strange man he is, she thought. To play music when he might die tomorrow.

But then she understood. He would have said that's the best time for it—when you know that it may be your last chance ever to play. And then she slept.

CHAPTER FIVE

Remember the Alamo!

THE FIRST THING Maria heard the next morning was also music—but it was the distant sound of trumpets and drums.

Mama heard it too. She put her arms around Maria and held her tightly.

"What does it mean?" Maria asked.

"It is *Le Degüello*—the Death Song," whispered Mama. "Santa Anna is telling us that he intends to kill everyone."

Maria looked up through the broken rafters of the church. The sky was still nearly dark, but red streaks showed that the sun was rising.

Then the cannons roared all around them like the loudest thunder she had ever heard. She felt the balls strike the fort. Then everyone began to scream. The smaller children cried out in terror, and up above she could hear the shouts of Crockett's men. Rifle shots cracked out, and finally the Alamo's cannons began to fire back.

The noise became so deafening that Maria could no longer think. Some of the women inside the chapel knelt in prayer. Others, like Mama, tried to comfort the children. Some merely wept. Maria held José, who kept shouting in her ear, asking her what was happening outside.

But those inside the church could see nothing. They could only try to listen to the sounds of the battle. Maria lost all track of time, but at some point the cannonballs stopping hitting the fort. Then the shouts above became mixed with the cries of men shouting over and over, "Santa Anna!" She knew that the Mexicans were now trying to climb the walls. She felt sorry that she had not made more powder loads for Crockett.

From the other side of the church, where the plaza was, many rifles began to fire, and she heard the clang of swords striking. It could only mean that Santa Anna's men were inside the fort. They must have come over the north wall, where Travis had led the defenders.

Suddenly, Captain Dickinson came down the ladder from above. His wife rushed to him, carrying her baby. He picked up a bag of gunpowder and turned to her. "The Mexicans are inside the walls!" he shouted, and then started up the ladder with a last look at his wife and baby. "If they spare you, save our child," he called. Then he disappeared from sight.

The next time they heard his cannon fire, it was aimed in the other direction—not outside the walls, but inside. He was firing into the jumble of fighting men, hoping to drive the Mexicans out.

For a while, the fighting in the plaza moved farther away. Travis's men had fallen back inside the barracks where they slept and ate. Captain Dickinson's cannon was still firing. In between its shots, while the men were reloading the gun, Maria thought she heard Crockett's voice. Rifle shots still rang out from his direction. For a moment, she had hope that perhaps they might win after all.

But then cannonballs began to strike the walls of the church again. They came from inside the fort now. The Mexicans had captured some of the defenders' cannons and were aiming them at the last stronghold.

A loud crash came from the front door of the church, which was held shut with a steel bar. As Maria watched, the heavy wooden doors began to splinter. A hole opened, and she could see Mexican soldiers with a battering ram striking the door.

Some of the men from the roof came down the ladder. She did not see Captain Dickinson with them. As the double doors fell open with a crash, the Alamo's defenders fired at the Mexicans who rushed through.

The women and children ran back to a far corner of the church. From there Maria saw the defenders fall. Mexican soldiers stabbed at their bodies with bayonets. The Mexicans rushed forward without noticing the women, and began to swarm up the ladder.

The doorway was open and empty now. Maria looked at Mama and pointed. "We could run," Maria said. But Mama grabbed her and held her back.

The sounds from outside began to change. The rifle shots dwindled away. Shouting men ran by outside the doorway, but they were all Mexicans. The cannon on the roof had fallen silent. And Maria heard no more shots from the wall where Crockett's men had stood.

Another man stepped into the doorway. His bright blue coat showed he was a Mexican officer, and he had his sword drawn. He walked slowly inside, followed by half a dozen soldiers. They carried rifles with long sharp bayonets on the ends.

They peered into the dark corners of the church. Maria saw the officer's dark eyes stop when he saw them. He walked forward with his men following. Maria heard Mama and the other women begin to pray. The soldiers stood over them, pointing their bayonets, and Maria held her breath. She wanted to close her eyes, but every muscle in her body was frozen.

Then the officer waved his hand, and the bayonets lowered. "What are you doing here?" he said. No one answered.

He led them outside. Maria shrank from the sights she saw there. Bodies were lying everywhere. She recognized many of them, but there were many more white-coated Mexicans among the dead. Mexican soldiers walked through the fort, searching for anyone left alive. But all the Texans were dead.

As they passed the building where Jim Bowie's room had been, she saw the painting. It was lying discarded and torn in the dirt outside.

Someone had carried it here and then put a foot through it. She tried to break away, but one of the guards grabbed her roughly and pushed her back. It didn't matter, she told herself. She wouldn't have wanted to see what they had done to Bowie.

Outside the fort she looked for some sign of Crockett. A great heap of Mexican bodies lay beneath the wall where he had stood. She knew he had made them pay dearly for his life. She turned away, trying not to think that he must be dead too.

She looked up and saw the sun still low in the sky. She realized with surprise that it was still early morning. The battle, which had seemed so long inside the church, had really lasted only about an hour and a half. In that time all the defenders of the Alamo had given their lives. Why? Why? she kept asking herself.

The guards took them back to town and threw them into a little room. They waited for hours, not knowing what would happen next. Finally, the officer reappeared and marched them into the main square.

There, on a white horse, sat a man in the most splendid uniform she had ever seen. Gold and silver braid covered the collar and shoulders of his blue coat, and dozens of medals were pinned across his chest. His sword hung from his side in a scabbard of pure gold. The saddle and reins of his horse glittered with gold as well. She knew he must be Santa Anna.

He looked over the little group of women and children and sneered contemptuously. His eyes stopped as they met Maria's. She refused to look away, wanting him to see how much she hated him. He took a gold snuffbox from his pocket and put a pinch of tobacco into his nose. He sniffed and tossed his head.

"Traitors," he said in a loud voice. "I am sparing your worthless lives." One of the women fell to her knees.

"Not because you deserve to live," he said. "But because I want you to carry a message." He pointed to a wagon that stood nearby. "Go out of this place and tell the other rebels what you have seen. Tell them how Santa Anna treats those who dare to raise their arms against him. Tell them—they must surrender or die." He wheeled his horse around and trotted away.

Maria and the others climbed into the back of the wagon. Mama and Mrs. Dickinson sat up on the driver's seat. When the soldiers slapped the rump of the horse, the wagon lurched forward.

Maria looked back as they left San Antonio and saw smoke coming from the Alamo. Santa Anna's men were burning it.

The survivors of the Alamo traveled all day, heading for the town of Gonzales. Before they got there, three riders appeared in the distance. As they drew nearer, Maria sat up and shaded her eyes. She could barely believe what she saw, and leaped down from the wagon, running forward.

"Papa!" she shouted.

Papa and the other riders took them back to Gonzales. People rushed up, wanting to know what had happened at the Alamo. Maria saw their shocked faces as they heard the story.

She stood up. Something had been burning within her ever since she had seen Santa Anna. She remembered her promise to Jim Bowie. "Don't give up!" she shouted. "Remember Jim Bowie! Remember Davy Crockett! Remember the Alamo!"

Maria's cry echoed and re-echoed—all through Texas and back to the United States. To Louisiana, where many of the Alamo's defenders had come from. To Tennessee, whose people wept at the news of Crockett's death.

And from all those places, and many more, people came to help the Texans fight Santa Anna. For the news of the Alamo did not make them afraid, as Santa Anna had hoped. It made them angry.

Maria saw Santa Anna one more time, only forty-six days after the Alamo had fallen. On April 21, Houston's army, strong now, finally attacked. At the San Jacinto River, the Texans overran Santa Anna's camp and completely destroyed his army.

Santa Anna fled. He threw off his fine uniform and disguised himself in the clothes of an ordinary soldier. But the Texans found him and dragged him back to Sam Houston, who had been wounded in the battle.

Maria was there and saw fear in the eyes of the man who had burned the Alamo. She stepped out of the crowd that had gathered. She looked right at him, but couldn't be sure if he recognized her. "I was at the Alamo," she said softly. "Jim Bowie and Davy Crockett were my friends."

Long after Texas won its freedom, she told the story and never let anyone forget them. And no one ever has.

MAKING
A PIÑATA

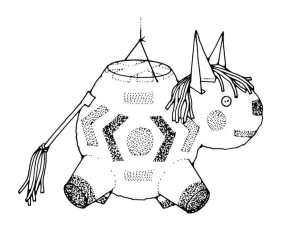

THE CUSTOM of making a piñata began in Italy during the 1500s. Italians called the clay jars they used *pignàttas*, which comes from the Italian word *pígna*, meaning "cone-shaped." The idea spread to Spain, where the word for it became *piñata*. Spaniards brought the custom to their colonies in Latin America. Today, breaking a piñata as part of a celebration has spread throughout many other countries, including the United States.

Maria and her friends made their piñatas from clay jars, baked so they were thin enough to be broken easily. It is easier to make one from the materials listed below.

Materials Needed

Balloons, Newspapers, Flour and water, Scissors, String, Paint and brush.

Steps

1. Cut the newspapers into strips about an inch wide.
2. Blow up the balloon and tie it.
3. Make a paste by mixing one part flour to two parts water.
4. Paste the paper strips onto the balloon. Leave a hole at the top so that you can fill the piñata later. Make the strips about four or five layers thick, so the piñata will not be too easy to break.

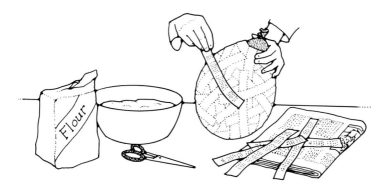

5. Let the paste dry overnight.

6. Break the balloon with a pin. The piñata should now be sturdy enough to fill with small fruit, candy, toys, and trinkets.

7. With the scissors, make two small holes near the top of the piñata. Run a string through them to use in hanging the piñata.

8. Fill the piñata. Then paste several more strips of paper or cardboard across the hole. Make sure when you hang the piñata that this part is at the top.

9. Decorate the piñata. Besides paint, you can use such things as colored paper, cloth, buttons, or paper cups. Use your imagination!

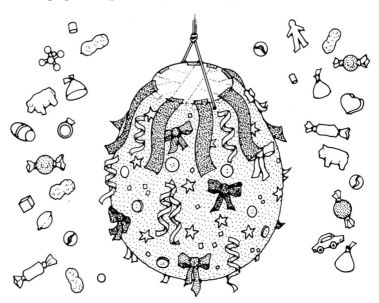

Tips

With practice, you can make more elaborate piñatas. For example, use two balloons—a small one for a head and a larger one for a body. Connect them by pasting newspaper strips between them. You can also begin with a thin cardboard box instead of a balloon.

Rubber cement is better than paste for attaching colored paper and other materials to the piñata.

Make sure everyone stands out of the way when a blindfolded guest is swinging a stick at the piñata!

ADDITIONAL TITLES AVAILABLE IN THE **HER STORY** SERIES,

by Dorothy and Thomas Hoobler:

Read the story of . . .

Sarah Tsaluh Rogers in
The Trail on Which They Wept:
The Story of a Cherokee Girl
By Hoobler & Hoobler/Burrus
LSB 0-382-24331-5
jh/c 0-382-24333-1
s/c 0-382-24353-6

Amy Elizabeth Harris in
Treasure in the Stream:
The Story of a Gold Rush Girl
By Hoobler & Hoobler/Carpenter
LSB 0-382-24144-4
jh/c 0-382-24151-7
s/c 0-382-24346-3

Maria Hernandez in
A Promise at the Alamo:
The Story of a Texas Girl
By Hoobler & Hoobler/Hewitson
LSB 0-382-24147-9
jh/c 0-382-24154-1
s/c 0-382-24352-8

Annie Laurie MacDougal in
The Sign Painter's Secret:
The Story of a Revolutionary Girl
By Hoobler & Hoobler/Ayers
LSB 0-382-24143-6
jh/c 0-382-24150-9
s/c 0-382-24345-5

Fran Parker in
And Now,
a Word from our Sponsor:
The Story of a Roaring '20's Girl
By Hoobler & Hoobler/Leer
LSB 0-382-24146-0
jh/c 0-382-24153-3
s/c 0-382-24350-1

Emily in
Next Stop, Freedom:
The Story of a Slave Girl
By Hoobler & Hoobler/Hanna
LSB 0-382-24145-2
jh/c 0-382-24152-5
s/c 0-382-24347-1

Laura Ann Barnes in
Aloha Means Come Back:
The Story of a World War II Girl
By Hoobler & Hoobler/Bleck
LSB 0-382-24148-7
jh/c 0-382-24156-8
s/c 0-382-24349-8

Christina Ricci in
Summer of Dreams:
The Story of a World's Fair Girl
By Hoobler & Hoobler/Graef
LSB 0-382-24332-3
jh/c 0-382-24335-8
s/c 0-382-24354-4

"This is a well-written and informative series with believable characters."
— American Bookseller "Pick of the Lists"

For price information or to place an order, call toll-free 1-800-848-9500.